For Murphy
—G. W.

For Marmalade
—E. S.

SIMON & SCHUSTER BOOKS FOR YOUNG READERS
An imprint of Simon & Schuster Children's Publishing Division
1230 Avenue of the Americas, New York, New York 10020
Text copyright © 2014 by Gene Weingarten
Illustrations copyright © 2014 by Eric Shansby
SIMON & SCHUSTER BOOKS FOR YOUNG READERS is a trademark of Simon & Schuster, Inc.
For information about special discounts for bulk purchases, please contact Simon & Schuster Special Sales
at 1-866-506-1949 or business@simonandschuster.com.
The Simon & Schuster Speakers Bureau can bring authors to your live event. For more information
or to book an event, contact the Simon & Schuster Speakers Bureau at 1-866-248-3049
or visit our website at www.simonspeakers.com.
Book design by Laurent Linn
The text for this book is set in Shansby Kid.
The illustrations for this book are rendered digitally.
Manufactured in China
0714 SCP
2 4 6 8 10 9 7 5 3 1
Library of Congress Cataloging-in-Publication Data
Weingarten, Gene.
Me & dog / Gene Weingarten ; illustrated by Eric Shansby.—First edition.
pages cm
Summary: For one dog, a boy is his everything.
ISBN 978-1-4424-9413-8 (hardcover : alk. paper)
ISBN 978-1-4424-9414-5 (eBook)
[1. Stories in rhyme. 2. Dogs—Fiction.]
I. Shansby, Eric, illustrator. II. Title. III. Title: Me and dog.
PZ8.3.W4243Me 2014
[E]—dc23
2013006448

Me & Dog

Gene Weingarten

ILLUSTRATED BY Eric Shansby

SIMON & SCHUSTER BOOKS FOR YOUNG READERS

NEW YORK LONDON TORONTO SYDNEY NEW DELHI

This is me.
My name is Sid.

I'm just an
ordinary kid.

I make ~~misteaks.~~
mistakes

They're mostly small,
except for when they're not . . .

. . . at all.

This is Murphy.
He's my pet.

He's the world's best dog, I bet.

But just between us, me and you . . .

Murphy's ordinary, too.

Murphy's pretty smart, but he thinks a bit too much of me.

To him, I'm not a short grade-schooler.

Super-duper

boss

and king

of absolutely

So yesterday, while getting mail,

oops!

I stepped on Murphy's tail.

He yelped then blinked
his big, brown eyes

and started to . . .
apologize!

Murphy thinks
when things go
bad,

he must have
somehow made
me mad.

Happy things get understood

as his reward for being good.

I sometimes think
there *is* no boss—

that most
things happen
just . . . because.

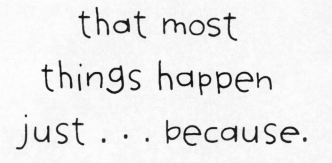

Murphy, though,
does not agree—

he sits around and
worships *me!*

He thinks that if
he begs enough,

I will give him
lots of stuff—

bits of beef and chunks of cheese,

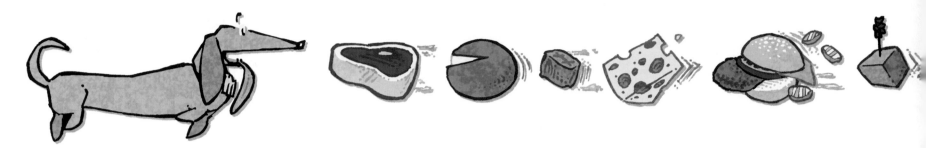

things to chase and

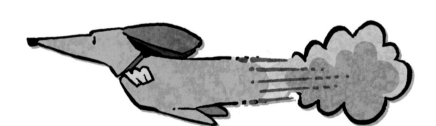

things to squeeze,

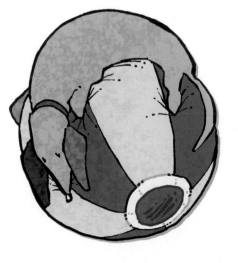

things to
honk

and things to shove,

and things
that only dogs
could love.

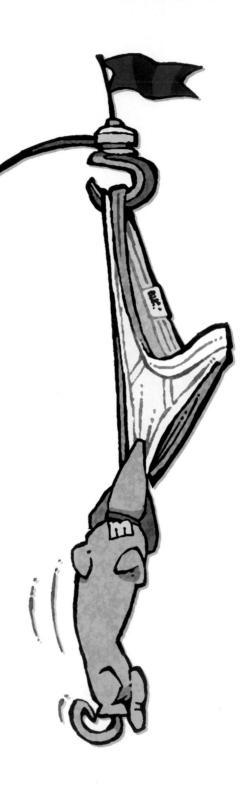

It's silly how he prays and pleads,

since I give Murphy all he needs.

Because he doesn't want me mad,
Murphy tries to not be bad.

And he isn't,
I admit.

(Except for when
he is, a bit.)

I wonder if he'd
be as good

if Murphy ever
understood

that I am *not*
the lord and king

of absolutely

everything.

I wonder if he
might be fearful

or less friendly

or less
cheerful

if he knew I'm
not the Wiz
(and maybe even
no one is).

So let's not tell him I'm just Sid,
a very ordinary kid.

It seems to work out perfectly

'cause I love him

and he loves me.